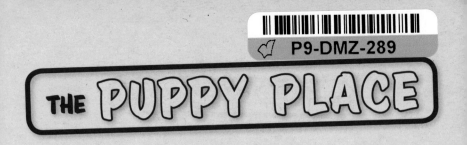

THE PUPPY PLACE

BOOMER

**Don't miss any of these
other stories by Ellen Miles!**

THE PUPPY PLACE

BOOMER

ELLEN MILES

SCHOLASTIC INC.

To Risë, Annie, and Joy

No part of this publication may be reproduced, stored in a retrieval system, or transmitted in any form or by any means, electronic, mechanical, photocopying, recording, or otherwise, without written permission of the publisher. For information regarding permission, write to Scholastic Inc., Attention: Permissions Department, 557 Broadway, New York, NY 10012.

ISBN 978-0-545-72644-3

Cover art by Tim O'Brien
Original cover design by Steve Scott

12 11 10 9 8 7 6 5 4 3   15 16 17 18 19 20/0

Printed in the U.S.A.   40

First printing, September 2015

CHAPTER ONE

"Did you wipe your feet?" Mom frowned as she pointed to Lizzie's sneakers.

Lizzie sighed. "Yes, I wiped my feet. And I'm barely even inside, anyway! I just came back for another load." She held out her arms, and her mom piled them full: a small cooler, a rolled-up sleeping bag, a pillow. Lizzie staggered back out into the driveway to hand it all over to her dad, who was packing the van.

"I can't wait to set up our campsite!" she said as she passed the sleeping bag to Dad. "I hope it has a good view of the lake." This was going to be a special trip: a three-day weekend with just Dad and Lizzie and her two younger brothers, Charles and the Bean. And Buddy, of course. How could they leave their adorable puppy behind? They were going camping at Crystal Lake, and they were going to hike and fish and make s'mores and play cards. Mom was really missing out. Not that Mom minded, Lizzie knew. She had plans of her own.

It was time for Mom's annual Fab Four reunion, when she got together for a long weekend with three of her best friends from college. Sometimes they met at a spa or a hotel, but this time "the girls" were coming to the Petersons' house. They'd been there once before, when Lizzie was only five or six years old. She didn't remember much about their visit except that Annie had a loud voice, Risa smelled good, and Joy had brought her a present, a horse doll with a beautiful golden coat and a white mane. Lizzie still had that palomino, the only horse among all the dog figurines on her shelf. There had also been a lot of laughter. Lizzie remembered that. The "girls" were always laughing. Risa's laugh was especially memorable: she sounded like a donkey braying, which always made everyone else laugh even more.

Now the girls were about to arrive for a three-day visit. Mom, who didn't normally care so much about people wiping their feet, had been cleaning for weeks. She had bought bright new curtains for the living room, and fluffy new towels, and pretty little soaps that smelled like coconut, raspberry, and lemon. The house was glowing, with everything in its place. Lizzie and Charles had cleaned their rooms, and Lizzie had helped put clean sheets on all the beds, including the pullout couch in the den. Every closet and shelf was neat and tidy. There was even a bouquet of sweet-smelling yellow roses on the dining room table.

"I just want our house to look nice," Mom said every time Dad told her to take it easy. "The girls haven't been here in a long time."

Now, as they packed up the van, Mom piled another load into Lizzie's arms and handed Charles a dog bowl and a dog bed. "Don't forget Buddy's things," she said.

Buddy was already sitting in the van, ready to go. The little brown pup loved adventures, as long as they involved his favorite people. Each time Lizzie brought out a load, she petted him, rubbing the heart-shaped white spot on his chest. She loved Buddy so much, and she felt so lucky that he had found his way to her family.

The Petersons helped puppies who needed

homes. They kept the dogs for only a short time, until they figured out the perfect home for each puppy. The hardest part of being a foster family was giving up the puppies when the time came — and in Buddy's case it had been impossible. The Petersons had agreed that he was part of their forever family, and he had come to stay.

Even Mom (who was more of a cat person, really) was crazy about Buddy. Still, Lizzie knew that she would be happy to have Buddy out of the house for the weekend. He was a good boy who never made messes or chewed things up, but after all, a puppy was a puppy. He might get excited with new people around. He might jump on her guests or try to run off with someone's shoe.

"It's a good thing you're coming with us," Lizzie told him the next time she went out to the van. "You'll have much more fun on our camping trip, anyway." Buddy licked her hand and sighed happily, settling into the dog bed Dad had set up for him in the van's way-back. He looked cozy, curled up amidst all the camping gear piled high around him.

Lizzie couldn't wait to get going. She could practically smell the fresh, piney air they would be breathing, and see the sparkly lake. After all that cleaning, it would be a relief to live in a tent for a few days. "Come on," she urged Dad. "Don't we have enough stuff? Look at it all!"

"That's exactly what I'm doing." Dad had a clipboard in his hands, and he was ticking things off the packing checklist he had made. "Camp stove, tent, big cooler, little cooler. Check, check, check, check. Lizzie, did you remember to pack the Bean's toothbrush and a couple of his favorite books?"

Lizzie nodded. "They're all in his backpack. Can we go now?"

Mom came out on the back stairs and stood with her arms folded, looking a little impatient. "The girls will be here any minute," she said.

Lizzie could guess what Mom really meant but was too nice to say: "Please get going — now!"

"Okay, okay," said Dad. "I get the message. Time to go." He hugged Mom. "We won't have cell service, but you have the phone number at the campground if there's an emergency, right?"

"Got it," Mom said.

"Not that I expect any emergencies," Dad said. "But you never know what kind of shenanigans the Fab Four might get up to."

Mom giggled. "We're just going to have a nice, quiet weekend catching up with each other. We're all grown up now."

Lizzie had heard stories about some of the silly stunts the Fab Four had pulled. They had all been good students who'd gotten excellent grades, but they were also famous for having fun. They had done things like filling a friend's entire dorm room with crumpled-up newspaper while she was at a class, and changing the letters on a sign at the local ice cream stand so instead of ICE CREAM CONES it said SCARE MICE ONCE. They had driven cross-country, and they'd gone swimming in a fountain at midnight, and they'd danced until their shoes wore out. Lizzie believed the stories, but she couldn't quite imagine her mom doing things like that.

She ran to her mom and threw her arms around her. "Love you," she said. "Bye!"

The Bean stared at Mom, as if he was just realizing that she was not going with them. He clung to her legs. "Please come, Mommy!" he wailed.

Mom sighed and bent down to hug him. "I'll miss you, Beanie," she said. "But I'm staying here. You'll have fun with Daddy."

The Bean wailed louder.

Lizzie heard the phone ringing inside. "I'll get it," she said, thinking she might grab a couple of the chocolate chip cookies Mom had baked for her visitors. A cookie would be the perfect distraction for the Bean. She ran into the kitchen and grabbed the phone. "Hello?" She heard barking on the other end of the line. "Hello?"

"Lizzie! I'm so glad I caught you." The woman's voice was tense, but Lizzie knew who it was: Ms. Dobbins, the director of Caring Paws, the animal shelter where she volunteered most Saturdays. "I need your help," said Ms. Dobbins. She sounded desperate. "I can't think of anyone else who could handle this puppy."

"Puppy?" Lizzie asked. The picture in her head — the one of a peaceful campsite under tall pines, near a silvery lake — popped like a soap bubble and disappeared. "What kind of puppy?"

CHAPTER TWO

"So it's a yes?" Ms. Dobbins asked. "Great. Wonderful. Perfect. I'm on my way."

Lizzie stared at the phone in her hands. She had not learned anything at all about the puppy. Without even answering a single question, Ms. Dobbins had hung up. Lizzie guessed that Ms. Dobbins needed her to foster a puppy. She had not said yes — though she'd been about to ask Mom if she could. Lizzie always wanted to say yes to puppies.

"Who was that?" Mom asked, coming in from the kitchen. "Better hop into the van. The engine's on and Dad is waiting."

Lizzie shook her head. "I don't think I'm going camping," she said.

Mom raised her eyebrows. "Oh, no?" she said. "And why not, may I ask?"

"Because Ms. Dobbins needs my help." Lizzie looked down at the floor to avoid her mom's eyes.

"Your help? With what?"

Lizzie's family had fostered lots of puppies from Caring Paws. Did she really have to explain what "helping" Ms. Dobbins meant? Even without looking up, Lizzie knew that her mother was frowning.

Mom groaned. "Oh, no. Don't tell me. You didn't —"

"I didn't!" said Lizzie. "I know I'm not supposed to agree to fostering a puppy before talking to you. But Ms. Dobbins just hung up on me before I could say a word."

"I don't care," said Mom. "Call her back. Tell her you can't. She'll have to find someone else."

Lizzie kicked her sneaker into the floor. "I can't." Her voice was almost a whisper. "She's on her way." She looked up at her mom. "I promise I will do everything. Walks, food, whatever it takes to help this puppy. You and your friends won't even know we're here. I'll sleep on the floor in your office. Just let me get my air mattress and sleeping bag out of the van."

Mom sank into a chair. "I can't believe this is happening," she said.

"Please, Mom?" Lizzie begged. "Ms. Dobbins needs to know that she can depend on us — you've said it yourself. That's just part of being a foster family. Right? Please, Mom?"

Mom sighed and nodded. "You're right. We've made a commitment and I suppose we have to follow through when we're needed." She threw up her hands. "Fine. Whatever. I surrender. Get your stuff."

Lizzie grinned. She was sorry to miss the camping trip, but there was no question about it: she would much rather meet a new puppy. A new foster puppy! And she was the only one Ms. Dobbins could turn to. That made Lizzie feel good.

She ran out to the van and explained quickly as she poked through their gear, looking for her things. Mom came out, too, and she and Dad had a whispered conversation.

"Hold on, hold on," said Dad as Lizzie pulled out her sleeping bag and her backpack. He turned off the van and got out to help Lizzie. "I hope you're not making a mistake. You're missing out on a fun trip."

"How can it be a mistake?" Lizzie asked. "It's a puppy!"

"Just make sure the puppy doesn't ruin Mom's weekend," said Dad. "She's really been looking forward to having this time with her friends."

"I will," Lizzie promised. She gave him a big hug and waved good-bye to him and her brothers as they drove off.

Inside, she piled her things in the front hall and looked around. Was there anything she needed to do to puppy-proof the house? Buddy was past his chewing phase (and, of course, his "accident" phase), so things had gotten a little more relaxed. She noticed Dad's slippers by his chair and scooped them up. They were way too tempting for a puppy who liked to chew. Lizzie stopped for a second. She didn't even know how old this puppy was! Or whether it was a girl or a boy, what size and breed it might be . . . She knew nothing, nothing at all. She felt her heart beat faster. What could be more exciting than this?

Lizzie went into the kitchen to make sure that the garbage was safe inside the cabinet under the sink, a clean bowl full of fresh water was on the dog-bone-shaped rubber place mat, and no tempting nibbles were within reach. She nodded and crossed her arms. Everything looked ready.

Mom dashed in, checking her watch. "What time did Ms. Dobbins say she would be here? The girls are going to arrive any second." She rearranged a bunch of lemons and limes in a bowl in the middle of the kitchen table, then grabbed a sponge to wipe down the already shining counters.

"I'll take care of everything," Lizzie promised again. "You won't have to worry about a thing."

Now Mom was checking her reflection in the stainless-steel refrigerator. "Why does my hair have to look like this, today of all days?" she muttered.

Lizzie wrapped her arms around her mother's waist. "You look beautiful," she said. "Anyway, they're your best friends. They don't care how you look. They just want to be with you."

Mom nodded, as if she were hearing the words for the first time. Actually, Lizzie was just repeating what she'd heard her dad say over and over in the past few days. "I know, I know," Mom said. "But you know how Risa looks. She always has the greatest outfits, so pulled together and professional."

According to Mom, Risa was the most successful of her friends. She had her own business, an Internet start-up. She lived in Chicago but traveled all over the world and had met tons of famous people: movie stars, politicians, singers. She had even been in the newspaper, lots of times. Not little hometown papers, like the *Littleton News*, where Mom was a reporter. Big, famous newspapers that were read by everybody in the world.

"Who cares?" Lizzie tightened her arms around her mother. "You look better to me. I love you." This time she wasn't copying Dad. This time it came straight from her heart. "Anyway, it's not like your other friends are fashion superstars, from the pictures I've seen."

Annie, the friend who ran a ranch in Wyoming (Lizzie remembered hearing that she and her husband had, like, ten thousand cows, plus dogs, cats, chickens, and other assorted animals, along with three kids), mostly wore jeans and work shirts — maybe a belt with a silver buckle if she was dressing up. And Joy, the artist with the curly hair, always looked like she'd grabbed whatever was most colorful out of her closet and combined it with other colorful things from her drawers to create a big, happy, colorful, wearable mess.

Lizzie had to admit that she was sort of eager to meet the girls now that she was a little more grown up. She had the feeling they weren't like other adults she knew in Littleton. They were . . . interesting.

She heard a car pull up to the house and honk the horn. "That's Ms. Dobbins!" she said, at the same time Mom said, "That's the girls!" Mom ran to the back door to greet her friends as they pulled into the driveway, while Lizzie ran to check the front door, flinging it wide open in her excitement.

Lizzie turned out to be right. There on the porch was Ms. Dobbins, standing next to a puppy already bigger than Buddy, with huge blocky paws and a big blocky head and lots and lots and lots of shaggy brown and black hair. Without any warning, the puppy lunged past Lizzie, galloping full speed through the living room and into the dining room. Lizzie watched, her hands covering her mouth, as the puppy charged across the rug, then slid on the polished wood floor, scrabbling desperately in an attempt to put on the brakes.

The brakes failed.

The puppy slid straight into a leg of the table. The table rocked forward and back but did not fall. The vase on top of it rocked back and forth and *did* fall, breaking into a million pieces and spraying water and flower petals all over.

Then everything was quiet for a moment. A lone rose petal drifted through the air and the puppy trotted over to sniff it. Ms. Dobbins cleared her throat. "Meet Boomer," she said.

CHAPTER THREE

Lizzie didn't know whether to laugh or cry. On one hand, it really was kind of funny. On the other, it was a total disaster. Mom was going to freak out when she saw what the new puppy had done to her beautiful, clean house. "Uh-oh. Can we catch him?" she asked Ms. Dobbins.

"We can try." Ms. Dobbins began to walk very slowly and calmly toward the puppy. Lizzie followed her example. "Boomer," Ms. Dobbins called in a low, soft voice. "Look what I have for you." She held out a treat she'd fished from her pocket.

The puppy looked up for a moment, then went back to sniffing at the rose petal he had caught in his paw.

The door to the kitchen swung open. "What was that noi —" Mom stood there, openmouthed, staring at the mess. Then she switched her gaze to Lizzie. "Get it cleaned up," she said. "Now." She stepped back into the kitchen, and the door swung shut behind her.

Lizzie gulped. As Ms. Dobbins continued to coax Boomer to move toward her, Lizzie knelt down and began to pick up the bigger pieces of vase on the floor. It was important to get all the sharp, broken shards off the floor before Boomer stepped on one of them and cut his paw.

"Wow," she said. "This puppy sure can shed." The floor under the dining room table was already covered in brown and black hairs with, Lizzie now noticed, a few golden ones mixed in.

"He's nervous," Ms. Dobbins said. "Some dogs shed a lot when they're nervous."

Now Lizzie noticed that Boomer was panting. He had left the rose petal behind to walk back and forth, just out of Ms. Dobbins's reach. Lizzie knew that panting and pacing were also signs that a dog was stressed out.

Ms. Dobbins knelt down and opened her arms. "Come on, Boomer," she called. "I'm not going to hurt you."

Lizzie could barely see the puppy's eyes behind a fringe of brown fur, but she could imagine that they would be darting around, the way Buddy's did when you tried to catch him to give him a bath. She knelt down, too. It always helped to get lower, to be on a dog's level, if you wanted to make a connection.

"It's okay, Boomer," she said. "Nobody's mad at you." That wasn't strictly true, she knew.

Mom was furious. But still, was it Boomer's fault that the vase had been unsteady? Lizzie was sure that Mom would come around. After all, this big messy puppy also happened to be completely adorable.

Boomer wagged his tail the tiniest bit and ducked his big handsome head.

I'd sure like to get to know you. But I'm — I'm kinda shy.

"He's not dangerous, is he?" Lizzie asked. Boomer looked scared, and she knew that a frightened dog would sometimes bite.

"Not in the least." Ms. Dobbins crouch-walked a few steps closer. "He's a total pussycat. Unless someone messes with one of his siblings. He came to us as one of a litter. They'd been living outside on their own for a few months. Five hungry, cold, scared little puppies." She shook her head. "Poor things. Anyway, Boomer's the biggest, and he thinks it's his job to protect them. That's one of the reasons we can't keep him. He barks constantly, because he's sure that one of the other dogs, or a shelter worker, is going to attack his brothers and sisters. The other puppies will be much easier to place without Boomer making such a fuss every time someone comes to look at them."

"What a story," said Lizzie. "You're a hero, Boomer. You took care of your family." She inched closer.

"He's just not used to people," said Ms. Dobbins. "Or leashes, or collars, or dog beds, or kibble, or any of the things that most dogs see every day. But he's a sweetie pie as soon as he knows he can trust a person. In fact, he's a real lovebug once he gets to know you. Along with being starved for food, he was starved for affection."

"He has a lot to learn," said Lizzie. Her heart swelled. She knew she could teach this sweet boy all about how to be a regular dog. She could comfort him, too. He must be lonely without his brothers and sisters. She took one crouching step forward, then another, holding out her hand and murmuring Boomer's name.

Boomer panted, shook himself, and panted some more.

This is making me very, very nervous!

"Don't worry, honey," said Lizzie. "I just want to pet your pretty coat." His coat was not actually very pretty — it was tangled and matted and had burrs in it — but she could tell that it would be soft and shining once he got cleaned up. She reached out her hand just a little further and managed to touch the collar that was loosely buckled around his neck. Her fingers slipped, but then she got a firm hold. "Got him," she said. She held the big pup securely and petted him with her other hand, rubbing his jaw and scratching between his ears. She had never met a dog who didn't like that.

Boomer leaned into her, drooling onto her favorite jeans. He flopped a heavy paw onto her arm.

I surrender.

"Awww, what a good boy." Lizzie smiled at Boomer and took the chunky paw in her hand. It was wet and muddy. She looked down to see dark tracks meandering through the dog hair, water, flower petals, and pieces of vase that covered the floor. What a mess! She groaned just as the doorbell rang again.

This time it had to be the girls.

CHAPTER FOUR

Mom popped out of the kitchen and ran through the dining room toward the front door, frowning at the mess. "I'll answer the door," she said. "You just — just get that dog out of my sight!"

Lizzie looked at Ms. Dobbins and jerked her head toward the kitchen. "Let's take him in there," she said. "Maybe he's hungry or thirsty. Anyway, Mom's having company."

Ms. Dobbins picked up the last pieces of vase and swept the fallen flowers into her arms. She nodded. "Good plan."

Lizzie pulled gently on Boomer's collar. "Let's go, cutie-pie," she said.

He looked up at her with his chocolate-drop eyes. For the first time, he gave her a doggy grin, complete with a long string of drool dangling from his droopy jowls.

I could tell right from the start. You're a nice person. I can trust you.

He stood up — he practically came up to Lizzie's waist! — and trotted meekly next to her as she headed for the kitchen with Ms. Dobbins following her. Just as they pushed through the swinging door, she heard squeals and excited talking from the front hall. The girls had arrived.

"Don't mind the mess," she heard her mom say. "We just had a little . . . situation. But Lizzie's taking care of it."

As soon as Lizzie let go of his collar, Boomer ran straight for the bowl of water she had set down. He stuck a big paw into it and nearly knocked it over, then shoved his entire snout into it and slurped noisily, splashing water onto the nearby cabinets. "Boomer!" Lizzie said, laughing. "Mind your manners." He looked up at her, water flooding off his big, dark muzzle.

Eh? Manners? What are those?

"He's so cute," said Lizzie. "And funny."

"I'm glad you think so," said Ms. Dobbins. "In fact, I was counting on it. I can't think of anyone else who might be able to deal with this dog." She frowned. "I hope your mom is going to be okay with this."

Lizzie waved a hand. "She'll be fine," she said. "I'm going to do nothing all weekend but pay attention to Boomer. He won't get in any more trouble."

Ms. Dobbins raised her eyebrows, started to say something, then stopped.

"What breed is he, anyway?" Lizzie asked.

"Well, what do you think?" Ms. Dobbins crossed her arms. It was like a little test, a chance for Lizzie to show off how much she knew about dog breeds.

Lizzie cocked her head and looked at Boomer. "I'd say he's a mix. Maybe part Saint Bernard?" she said. "And some German shepherd, and" — she racked her brain, trying to remember a breed from her "Dog Breeds of the World" poster, giant dogs that were supposed to look sort of like lions — "Leonberger!" The name came to her out of the blue.

Ms. Dobbins smiled. "That's just about exactly what I was thinking. Maybe with a little Great Pyrenees thrown into the mix."

"Little?" Lizzie asked, laughing. So far, every dog they had mentioned was either large or giant. It was a sure bet that Boomer was going to be a very big boy.

Ms. Dobbins laughed, too. Then she caught sight of the clock on the stove. "Oh, my! I've got to run. Are you all set? He can eat Buddy's food for tonight, but tomorrow you'll need to pick up some large-breed puppy food. It's important that his bones develop well, since he's going to be big."

Lizzie nodded. "I'm sure we can find some." She let Ms. Dobbins out the back door, then turned to see Boomer slurping at the water dish again, with a spreading puddle all around his feet.

Mom picked that moment to come into the kitchen. She took one look at the water and rolled her eyes. "Lizzie," she began. Then she just shook her head. "Come meet the girls."

Lizzie set up the baby gate so Boomer would not be able to push through the kitchen door. She followed her mom into the living room. "Here's Lizzie," Mom said, introducing her to the three women.

"It can't be!"

"She's all grown up!"

"Lizzie, look at you!"

They looked just like they did in the pictures. The one who must be Annie, dressed like a cowboy, whooped and grinned. Joy, small and round and draped in purple and blue scarves, leapt up to throw her arms around Lizzie. Tall, thin Risa, in a pale pink suit and high heels, smiled and looked Lizzie up and down in a way that made her very self-conscious. She was sure Risa noticed the big drool stain on her jeans. "Hi," Lizzie said. She answered a bunch of questions about school, then finally dashed back into the kitchen when Mom gave her a nod. She knelt down and coaxed Boomer into her lap. "Dogs are so much easier than people," she said into his thick, furry neck.

She and Boomer hung out in the kitchen until Mom came in to get dinner ready, pulling a warmed pan of lasagna out of the oven and putting the finishing touches on a big bowl of salad.

"I'll help!" Lizzie said, jumping up. She and Boomer were both going to have to be on their best behavior for the rest of the weekend. Quickly, she mopped up the last of the mess on the dining room floor and helped Mom set the table. Boomer didn't even whine once as they went in and out of the kitchen, stepping over the baby gate each time.

The girls came to the table. Mom brought the salad out, opening the baby gate for Lizzie, who was carefully carrying the lasagna pan. "Here we go," said Mom. "Everybody's hungry, I hope?"

But before they got to the table, Boomer charged out of the kitchen.

Wait for me! I'm tired of being alone.

He raced after Lizzie and jumped up to put a paw on her arm, tipping the lasagna onto the floor. He skidded through the cheesy, tomatoey mess, then kept loping straight toward the table, ending by putting both gloppy red paws up onto Risa's perfectly pressed pink lap.

"Oh!" she gasped, looking down at her ruined skirt.

"Mmph," said Joy, trying to stifle a laugh.

"Ha, ha, ha!" Annie burst out with a loud guffaw.

Risa glared at them both while Mom stood wringing her hands helplessly.

The Fab Four reunion weekend was off to a terrific start.

CHAPTER FIVE

"You should have seen the look on Risa's face!" Lizzie was upstairs, on the phone with her best friend, Maria. She had managed to wipe most of the mess off Boomer's feet — even though he had acted as if the towel were some terrifying weapon attacking him — and hustle him away from the scene in the dining room. "She was really mad. And her fancy suit is probably ruined, even though Mom offered to take it to the cleaner's."

"I'm sure it didn't help that the others were laughing at her," said Maria.

"Or that they both petted him before I got him out of there," Lizzie said. Annie and Joy had not seemed worried at all about their clothes getting ruined. "Anyway, I can't wait for you to meet Boomer. You won't believe how big he is. I think he's grown since he got here. And he's so, so cute."

"Can you bring him along when we walk dogs?" Maria asked. Lizzie and Maria and two other friends had a dog-walking business, with lots of clients. They walked dogs every day after school and did some training, too.

"He's too nutso right now," said Lizzie. "And he needs my full attention, so it's a good thing we have a long weekend. Maybe by Tuesday he'll be ready."

"I want to see him before then," said Maria.

"Come over tomorrow," Lizzie said. "Mom and the girls are going to a spa for the whole day."

When she hung up with Maria, Lizzie turned her attention to Boomer. "I bet you could be ready to walk with us by Tuesday. You're kind of clumsy, but I can tell that you're smart underneath all that fur."

She took him down the hall to her room to look for a brush to groom him with. She knew she probably couldn't brush him that night — he was way too wild — but maybe if she got him used to the brush things would go better the next day. She heard a burst of laughter from downstairs, her mom's high, snorty laugh floating above the others. Good. Mom and her friends were still having fun.

Boomer trotted after her eagerly. He sure was a friendly pup. Even though he had not known many humans in his life, he seemed to like people. "Including the ones who aren't so crazy about your messy paws," Lizzie told him as they entered her room. "You'd better keep out of Risa's way for the rest of the weekend."

She closed the door of her room and poked through her closet, looking for the basket of grooming tools she kept for long-haired puppies. Buddy's short coat rarely needed more than a quick brushing, but Lizzie knew it was important to keep longer dog hair from tangling and matting. While he waited, Boomer sniffed everything in the room, from the dog figurines to the shelf of dog-training books to Lizzie's bedside table to —

"No, Boomer!" Lizzie popped out of the closet just in time to see Boomer hop onto her bed. He looked up at her with a puzzled frown, his dark brown eyes innocent.

Is there some sort of problem?

Lizzie sighed. This puppy really did not know anything, including the meaning of the word "no."

She dashed over to reach for his collar, but he leapt off the bed and galloped around the room with his long, fluffy tail held high. He knocked over a lamp and scattered a pile of books as he ran.

Oh, it's not so easy to catch me! Watch me run.

Lizzie chased him for a moment, then stopped. She knew that the worst way to try to catch a runaway dog was by chasing it. That just made dogs run faster. She turned around and faced the other direction, fishing in her pocket for one of the treats she always carried. "This way, Boomer," she said, mimicking the sweet, gentle voice Ms. Dobbins had used earlier. "See what I have for you?"

Boomer trotted over to sniff at the hand she

was holding out, grabbed the piece of jerky, and gobbled it down.

Lizzie found another piece in her pocket. He stretched out his neck to get it. "Uh-uh," Lizzie said. "You have to do something for it this time." Holding it up high, she moved the treat over his head. When he leaned back to watch it, he plopped down on his big haunches. "Yes!" Lizzie said. "Sit!" She gave him the treat.

After he gobbled it, Boomer looked steadily at her with his huge melty brown eyes as he held up a giant paw.

Got any more of those?

Lizzie laughed. "You just learned to sit, and now you want to shake, too? Okay, shake!" She reached out a hand to take his paw, then quickly gave him a treat. This was going to be one of the easiest dog-training jobs ever. Boomer was such a smart dog, and he wanted to please. If she could keep him focused, he would learn really fast. "I bet I could have you ready for a forever home by the end of the weekend," Lizzie told him. They worked on "sit" and "shake" for a while. Then Lizzie added "lie down."

He plopped down on her rag rug and let out a long sigh. Maybe he was finally settling down. "Great," she told him, giving him the last treat in her pocket. "Now try to stay there for a second, will you? I want to find that brush." She went back to the closet and began rummaging through a plastic tub full of leashes and harnesses.

Just as she found the brush, she heard the door to her room open. She turned to see Risa's horrified face. Mom's friend stood openmouthed in her stained pink skirt. She stared at Boomer, who lay on his back across the rumpled, stained, dog-hair-covered quilt on Lizzie's bed, all four furry feet in the air.

Lizzie had forgotten: for the weekend, this was not her room.

CHAPTER SIX

Lizzie yawned loudly as she helped Mom clear the breakfast dishes the next morning. It had been late by the time she had helped remake the bed for Risa, then found her own place to sleep, laying out her air mattress and sleeping bag in Mom's office. Boomer had gotten her up twice in the night, once for a pee and once just because he seemed to think there was something important to check out in the backyard. Lizzie didn't mind — she was used to getting up in the middle of the night for puppies — but she was sleepy.

"Are you sure you'll be okay?" Mom asked her for the fifteenth time. "You'll be on your own all day." Instead of the spa, Annie had talked the girls into a visit to the new water park about an hour away. Lizzie had felt a pang when she heard that — she was dying to try out their Super Slide — but Boomer was much more important.

"I'll be fine," Lizzie said. "Maria is coming over, and we can always call a neighbor if we need to."

So far, Boomer had been pretty good that day. It was true that he had shredded the morning newspaper before anyone could read it, and maybe he had made a bit of a mess at his food and water bowls. But he had also let Lizzie brush him for a little while and cut some of the worst snarls out of his hair. And he had mostly managed to stay out of Risa and Mom's way while managing to pick up a few belly rubs from Annie and Joy.

After Mom and the girls left, Lizzie took Boomer out to the fenced backyard. She wanted him to start getting used to a leash. First she let him run around the yard for a while. He had a lot of energy! The huge puppy galumphed from spot to spot, sniffing and wagging his gorgeous tail as he checked everything out.

"Boomer," Lizzie called. She coaxed him toward her with a treat, then showed him the leash she was holding. At first he backed away as if she were shoving a live snake into his face. He rolled his eyes and panted. "It's okay," Lizzie said. She worked with him, using treats and a very soft voice, until he could stand for her to clip the leash onto his collar. It took a lot of patience, but Lizzie saw right away that as long as she was gentle with him, Boomer could learn quickly. It only took her another ten minutes or so to teach him to come running when she called his name.

"Wow!" Maria appeared out on the deck. "He's huge!"

"Told you," said Lizzie. "Come meet him. Move slowly and gently, though. He gets spooked easily."

Maria tiptoed down the deck stairs to join Lizzie and Boomer on the lawn. "Hi, Boomer," she said, holding out the back of her hand for the puppy to sniff.

Boomer sniffed. Then he wagged his tail.

You're okay. I can tell. You smell like dog.

"He smells Simba," Maria said. Maria's mom was blind, and Simba, a big calm yellow Lab, was her guide dog. "He's really cute. Kinda scruffy, but cute."

"I brushed him this morning," Lizzie said. "I think he would look a whole lot better if he had a bath."

She looked at Maria.

Maria looked at her.

"Want to?" Lizzie asked. Until that moment, she had not planned to give Boomer a bath that day — but suddenly it seemed like a great idea.

"I don't know," said Maria. "What about your mom's company? The girls?"

Lizzie thought of Risa's face when she had seen the filthy bed. It sure was hard to picture her swooping down a giant waterslide and landing with a splash. "It'll be fine," she said. "Even if things get a little messy, we'll have plenty of time to clean up before they get home."

It took a while to round up all the things they would need: the Bean's baby shampoo, some plastic cups to use for rinsing Boomer off, a stack of old but clean towels from the back of the closet in the hall. Lizzie put the heater on in the bathroom so it would be nice and cozy, and ran a few inches of warm water into the tub. Finally, they were ready. She coaxed Boomer into the bathroom with some Swiss cheese she had found in the fridge. "My secret weapon," she told Maria as she closed the door to trap him inside. "No dog can resist cheese. They'll do anything for it."

Anything but get into a tub of water. Even when Maria and Lizzie tried lifting him in together, Boomer struggled and squirmed and stuck his chunky legs out straight and squirted out of their grip and skidded around the room, rumpling up the bath mat and knocking bottles and jars off the sink as he tried to find an escape route.

"Poor puppy," said Maria. "He's so scared. Maybe we should just try another day."

Lizzie had caught Boomer. She sat on the floor and held him half on her lap, half off, petting him and calming him down. "We've gotten this far," she said, panting a little. "Let's not quit now."

Finally, the girls managed to wrestle Boomer into the tub and get him soaked with water. "He looks so much smaller," said Maria.

"Skinny, too," said Lizzie. She was surprised by the way his ribs stuck out when his fluffy coat didn't hide them. Suddenly, it was easier to picture him and his siblings living on their own in the wild. Poor Boomer. He'd been through a lot in his short life.

Once he was wet, Boomer seemed to give up the fight. He let them massage soap into his fur and even stood quietly, shivering a little, while they rinsed it out.

This almost feels . . . good!

Lizzie and Maria poured cups of warm water over Boomer, making sure not to get it into his eyes. "I think we've got most of it," Lizzie said, just as the huge puppy decided he'd had enough. He leapt out of the tub and bounced around the bathroom again, shaking off soapsuds and water. When Lizzie began to towel him off, he ran away and tried to hide behind the toilet.

"Let's take him outside," she said. "It's not too cold out, and he'll dry off if he runs around. I think he looks much better, don't you?"

"He does," said Maria. "But I'm not so sure about this room." Lizzie followed her eyes and saw the rumpled, wet towels, the clumps of brown and black hair, the water and soap spattered everywhere, and the towel rack that had been pulled halfway off the wall.

Lizzie giggled. "It's pretty bad," she agreed. "I'll

take care of it later. Let's get this guy dry and work some more on his training."

By the time Mom and the girls got home, Boomer looked beautiful. His coat was sweet-smelling and fluffy, and the gold hairs shone brightly against his dark fur. The hours had flown by as Lizzie and Maria worked with him in the yard, and all the training paid off. He had learned to walk on the leash without pulling — at least for a few steps — and his sit and shake were almost perfect.

Annie and Joy rushed out to see him. They cooed over him as they petted his soft coat, and Lizzie was proud — until she heard a screech from upstairs. "Oh, no," she said, putting her hand over her mouth.

How could she have forgotten to clean up the bathroom?

CHAPTER SEVEN

Once again, Annie and Joy seemed to think the whole thing was kind of funny. They stood at the door of the bathroom, hands over their mouths, giggling as they took in the mess. Risa, who was wearing only a towel, obviously did not think it was the least bit amusing. "I'm freezing to death from the cold water at that silly park," she said, shivering. She marched out of the room, muttering under her breath.

Lizzie made a face like "Isn't she snooty?" but Annie shook her head. "Don't mind her," she said. "Risa works too hard at a job she doesn't really love. She's a country girl at heart, but she's living in a city, and she's a homebody who has to travel all the time."

Joy nodded. "I've never seen her so unhappy. Remember how she used to laugh all the time? With that sound like a donkey braying? It's obvious that she has to change her life. But I don't see that happening anytime soon." She shrugged and waved a hand at the mess in the room. "Want some help with this?" she asked Lizzie.

"That's okay," said Lizzie. "It was my idea to give Boomer a bath."

"I think he really needs some exercise, maybe some playtime with other dogs," said Annie. "Is there a dog park around here?"

Lizzie thought a trip to the dog park sounded like a wonderful idea. Mom wasn't as crazy about it, but Annie could be very persuasive. "We'll take the van we rented. Plenty of room," she said.

Even Risa came along. "I'm not going to let a

silly puppy cheat me out of time with my friends," she said as she climbed into the van in her spotless white tracksuit.

Lizzie sat in the far backseat with Boomer next to her. She held tight to the big puppy's leash so he wouldn't jump on anyone. "You *are* a big silly," she whispered into his soft, silky ear. "But at least you're not dirty anymore. Not after that bath. And you're not really naughty, either. Or at least you don't mean to be. You just don't know any better. You can't help it."

Boomer licked her cheek, his huge tongue swabbing her face from bottom to top, and leaned against her.

I know I like you, that's for sure!

Lizzie hugged his big, sturdy body. "Good boy," she said. She was glad that Boomer seemed to trust her. It was hard to believe that he had been living on his own only a few days before. How had he and his siblings survived? Lizzie guessed that they had probably raided garbage cans for food, and found water in puddles and streams. They had lived like wild animals. How could anyone expect Boomer to have perfect manners after that?

Boomer loved the dog park. As soon as he spotted the other dogs zooming around in the fenced-in area, his ears went up and his tail began to wave. Mom and Risa sat on a bench beneath a tree outside the fence, but Annie and Joy followed Lizzie and Boomer through the gate. "Maybe I'd better hold on to him for a bit, just so we can see how he reacts to the other dogs," Lizzie said. It was a good thing she had spent some time getting Boomer used to being on a leash.

She looked around, trying to see how many dog breeds she could guess. She spotted a Pomeranian, a little orange ball of fluff who reminded her of Teddy, a puppy her family had fostered. He was playing with a Jack Russell terrier — a wiry-coated one, not a smooth-coated one like Rascal, another foster puppy. There were some big dogs, too: Labs and Lab mixes; a furry, wolflike malamute; and a very handsome cocoa-colored standard poodle. Lizzie figured that Boomer would want to play with the larger dogs, but when the Pom and the Jack Russell came over to sniff him, his tail wagged harder and harder as the three dogs said hello to one another. He gazed up at Lizzie with a pleading look in his chocolate-drop eyes.

May I please go play with my new friends?

"Think it's okay to let him run?" Lizzie asked.

"He seems fine," said Annie. "I don't see a single sign of aggression, like growling or baring his teeth. I think Boomer is just a sweet guy."

Lizzie unclipped the leash and Boomer took off running, galloping along with the smaller dogs trotting around him like two orbiting planets. Two yappy orbiting planets! Neither one of them stopped barking for a second, and Lizzie wondered how they could even breathe.

"Hey, look at that yellow Lab," Lizzie said. "He only has three legs but he can run as fast as the other dogs."

"A tripod," said Annie. "That's what some people call them. I used to have a three-legged dog. Good old Sam. He lost his leg when he was hit by a car, before I had him, but he could do anything the other dogs could do, and he was always in a happy mood. Dogs can adjust to almost anything."

"Boomer is already adjusting to being around people and other dogs," Lizzie said. She glanced at Annie, wondering if Mom's friend might be looking for a dog to adopt. She seemed to know a lot about animals, and Lizzie was sure that Annie's ranch would be an excellent forever home for any dog. She just had to find the right moment to bring the idea up.

For now, they sat and watched the dogs play, commenting on the silly things they did. Lizzie could have stayed at the dog park forever, but soon their time was up.

"Let's go," Mom called.

Boomer and the little dogs were wading in a blue plastic kiddie pool, splashing about in the chilly water. "Look at that," said Lizzie. "You wouldn't believe it's the same dog I had to wrestle into a warm bath." She clapped her hands. "Come on, Boomer!"

The big dog stopped when he heard his name. That was another thing he'd learned fast! He looked at Lizzie, paused for a moment as if he was deciding whether to obey, then galloped back toward her. Lizzie felt her eyes fill with tears. "What a good boy!" she said as she bent to pet him and clip on his leash. Boomer really did want to please. He gazed up at her happily and accepted the treat she handed him, then shook off from nose to tail, spraying her, Annie, and Joy with water.

"Sorry!" said Lizzie, even though they were both laughing. "I'll run ahead and get a towel from the back of the van. Better at least try to dry him off before he gets in." Boomer followed her, glancing back once or twice as if to say good-bye to his new friends.

The Fab Four were all in the van by the time Lizzie finished soaking up the worst of the muddy water clinging to Boomer's long shaggy coat. At least he wasn't as afraid of the towel this time. Until she tried to dry off his paws. Something about that terrified him, and he leapt away from her — straight into the van. He jumped up onto the seat, right between Annie and Risa, and buried his face in Risa's lap.

"Get him off!" Risa yelled.

Annie laughed. "It's only mud. It won't kill you. Look at those eyes! How can you be mad?"

Risa looked down into Boomer's face. She stopped squirming and yelling and just slumped in her seat. Lizzie offered to take Boomer into the backseat, but Risa shook her head. "It's fine," she said in a tired voice.

Lizzie sat down by herself in the backseat. Had she — and Boomer — ruined Mom's weekend with her friends?

CHAPTER EIGHT

"I'm so sorry." All the way home, Lizzie couldn't stop apologizing to Risa. "I don't know how he got away from me. I was trying to hold him. . . ."

Risa just shrugged. Boomer's head still lay on her lap. She seemed to have given up.

Annie looked back at Lizzie with a smile. "Don't worry, hon," she said. "Worse things have happened. She'll get over it. Anyway, I think you're real good with animals. You're kind and patient and a terrific little trainer. In fact" — she leaned a little closer — "maybe someday you'll come stay at the ranch for a little while, help us out. We can always use an extra young'un around the place.

And when you're a little older, you can even stay in the bunkhouse."

"The bunkhouse?" Lizzie pictured a long, low building packed with snoring, sleepy cowboys.

"Well, it used to be a bunkhouse, but now it's just our guest cabin. You'll see. It's adorable."

Lizzie felt her heart thump. How much fun would it be to live on a ranch and be a cowgirl? Maybe Maria could come, too. She loved horses. Best of all, maybe Lizzie would be seeing Boomer there. She had a feeling that it might not be too hard to convince Annie to adopt the big wild guy.

At home, Mom pulled Lizzie into the kitchen and shut the door. "I want you to keep Boomer away from everyone," she said.

"But Joy and Annie like him," Lizzie said. "Haven't you seen them giving him belly rubs?"

Mom shook her head. "I don't care," she said. "This weekend is for me and my friends. We only have a few days together every year, and I don't want them ruined. I'm afraid that one more incident might be too much for Risa, and I'd hate to see her leave early. It's not that she dislikes dogs — she's just stressed out and I don't think she likes having her expensive clothes ruined."

Lizzie nodded. She understood what Mom meant. It was obvious that Risa had just about had it with Boomer. And it seemed like every time the big dude was near her, he couldn't resist making the worst possible mess of her fancy outfit. "Okay," she said. "I'll do my best."

Mom nodded. "I know you will, honey." She checked the clock. "We have reservations for a special dinner at Chez Henri tonight. I don't like to leave you and Boomer alone again, but I can tell he's not ready to stay by himself, even in a crate."

"We'll be fine," Lizzie said. "We'll go play in the yard and I'll tire him out."

"And if there's an emergency —"

"I'll call the neighbors," Lizzie finished. "Really, don't worry."

"And there's still some lasagna left," Mom said. "Good thing I made two pans of it." She smiled at Lizzie.

Lizzie smiled back. Mom sure was a good sport for someone who wasn't originally much of a dog person. She had come a long way since they had first started fostering puppies.

Boomer seemed to be trying to climb inside his water bowl as he slurped noisily. "Come on, big boy," Lizzie said.

She and Boomer spent most of the afternoon in the backyard. First they played fetch. Lizzie worked on his manners as they played, using treats to teach him how to drop the ball into her hand when he brought it back — not that she really wanted to touch the disgusting thing. Boomer could take a brand-new tennis ball and turn it into a soggy, shredded mess in about five minutes.

"You do learn fast," Lizzie told him, putting the ball aside to dry in the sun for a few minutes. "How about 'lie down'? Remember how we worked on that one?" She knew that the more manners she taught him, the easier it would be to convince Annie to adopt this wild pup. She told him to sit; then, with a treat in her hand, she motioned to the ground, hoping he would follow her signal. Instead, he bent his head to try to get the treat from her.

"Uh-uh," said Lizzie. "You'll get the treat, but you have to lie down." She made the motion again. Boomer looked at her quizzically, his head tilted.

Aren't you going to give me the treat?

Lizzie suddenly had the sense that someone was watching from an upstairs window. She glanced up and saw a figure looking down at her and Boomer. Lizzie hoped it was Annie. She wanted to show off how quickly Boomer could learn. "Come on," she said to the dog. "You can do it. Down." She let Boomer smell the treat she held, then motioned again, moving her hand toward the ground.

This time, he settled down obediently. "Yes!" Lizzie cried as she handed him the treat. "Good boy." She glanced up, but the figure that had been at the window was gone. Boomer nudged her hand with his nose.

Got any more of those?

Lizzie laughed. "You're a terrific student," she said, scratching him between the ears. This wild child was already getting much more civilized.

"Lizzie!" her mom called from the back door. "Can you help me for a sec?"

Before Lizzie could even answer, Boomer ran to scoop up his ball, then galloped up the stairs of the deck and pushed past Mom, through the open door. "Wait!" Lizzie yelled.

"No!" Mom shouted.

But it was too late. By the time Lizzie and Mom made it into the living room, Boomer had already dropped the soggy ball into Risa's lap — Risa's very dressed-up lap, a lap that had been all ready for a special dinner at Chez Henri.

CHAPTER NINE

Lizzie could not believe it. Why couldn't Boomer just leave Risa alone? It was obvious that she was not in the mood for a big messy slobbery dog. "I'm so sorry," she said, for the fiftieth time that weekend, as she grabbed Boomer's collar and pulled him back toward the kitchen.

Mom stayed to talk to Risa. Lizzie heard bits of their conversation: Mom apologizing; Risa saying, in a sort of flat voice, that it didn't matter. "But I think I'll stay here tonight," she heard Risa say. "I don't really have another outfit to wear, and besides, I have some work I should do."

A moment later, Mom came into the kitchen. "Risa is —"

"I heard," said Lizzie.

"And please, just —"

"I know," said Lizzie. "Keep Boomer away from her. Got it."

Lizzie knelt down to put her arms around Boomer. "I know you don't mean to be naughty," she said into his ear. "You're just a little wild. You can't help it." Boomer panted and leaned into her, nuzzling her cheek with his wet nose.

You really understand me, don't you?

Annie and Joy were upset that Risa was not coming with them. "This restaurant is supposed to be great," said Joy, who looked like a gypsy in her long swirly purple velvet skirt.

"I eat in fancy restaurants all the time, with

my business clients," said Risa. "I'll be very happy eating leftovers."

Annie gave her friend a hug. "Don't work too hard," she said.

When they left, the house was suddenly very quiet. Quickly, Lizzie nuked a plate of lasagna and carried it up to Mom's study. She and Boomer could stay in there for the evening, and Risa could have the rest of the house. Risa could stay far away from the big puppy's muddy paws, slobbery jowls, and shedding coat.

Lizzie had eaten only one bite of lasagna when she heard a knock at the door. It was Risa. "You don't have to hide in here," she said. "Let's eat together."

"What about Boomer?" Lizzie asked.

"What more can he do to me?" said Risa. She waved a hand at the jeans she was wearing. "He's already ruined every outfit I brought. I had to borrow these from Annie, and we know she doesn't care about mud."

So Lizzie carried her plate back downstairs and sat in the kitchen with Risa, listening to stories about all the amazing places Risa had been. Boomer lay under the table with his head on Lizzie's feet, quiet and content after his own dinner. "You have a really cool life," Lizzie said after she heard about Risa's weekends in Paris and her trip to China.

Risa nodded. "I guess I do," she said. "I suppose I'm very lucky."

She was quiet for a few moments, and Lizzie thought she looked sad. She decided to change the subject. "Tell me about another Fab Four adventure. Mom tells the same stories over and over again."

"Did she ever tell you about the time — the *second* time — we all drove cross-country together?

There are plenty of stories from that trip I can tell you. Or maybe some of them I *shouldn't* tell you. Oh, my!" Risa sat back and let out a loud "hee-haw!"

Lizzie stared at her. It was incredible. She'd forgotten how much Risa really did sound like a donkey when she laughed.

"Oh," said Risa, meeting Lizzie's eyes. "I know, my laugh. It's ridiculous but I can't help it." She laughed again, and Lizzie could not resist laughing along with her. *That's what they mean when they say a laugh is contagious*, Lizzie thought. *You catch it, just like you can catch a cold.*

Lizzie saw Risa's hand drop toward the floor, where Boomer lay beneath the table. It came to rest on the puppy's big, blocky head. Lizzie's eyebrows shot up.

"What?" Risa asked. "Oh, you think I hate dogs. I don't! I love animals. I grew up on a farm, and we always had dogs. One golden retriever after another. They were my best friends. But there's no way I could have one now. I'm never home! It's just not fair to a dog." She looked sad again as she poked at the last bite of lasagna on her plate.

"It's funny," said Lizzie. "I always think that people who say that kind of thing would actually be the best dog owners, because they care."

As glamorous as Risa's life sounded, Lizzie thought she would rather have Annie's. Maybe Annie never got to go out to fancy restaurants or meet movie stars, but at least she could have dogs. And cows. And chickens.

"Maybe you could come on a trip with me sometime," Risa said. "I've taken my nieces all kinds of interesting places. And since the Fab Four are basically like sisters, you're pretty much my niece, too."

"Sure," said Lizzie. She loved adventures. "But not Paris. More like . . . maybe Iceland or the Amazon or somewhere."

They finished their dinner and moved into the living room, sprawling on opposite ends of the couch with Boomer nearby on the floor. "He's starting to settle in here," Risa said. "Maybe your mom will let you keep him."

Lizzie gasped. "Are you kidding?"

Risa hee-hawed. "Of course I am!" she said. "Your mom never was much of a dog person. I'm surprised you got to keep Buddy. Tell me all about him."

Lizzie told her all about Buddy, the best puppy ever. Risa listened and laughed and asked questions. She really was okay. Finally, Lizzie understood why Mom loved this friend so much. Boomer lay quietly, thumping his tail now and then and licking Risa's hand as she petted his huge furry head.

Maybe, Lizzie thought, the big messy dog had always sensed the truth about the "real" Risa that lay just beneath her dressed-up, in-control, businesswoman look. Maybe that was why he couldn't seem to stay away from her.

Maybe the big pup had fallen in love with the real Risa.

But could Risa ever fall in love with him?

CHAPTER TEN

Lizzie bolted upright in her sleeping bag. What was that horrible screeching sound? And where — she looked around wildly — was Boomer?

Then she remembered. The night before, she and Risa had talked for a long time. They had even watched part of a movie, but Lizzie had started yawning and had finally headed off to her temporary bed in Mom's study.

"You can leave Boomer with me," Risa had said. "He can keep me company while I work on this ridiculous report." She'd pulled a sheaf of papers out of her briefcase and settled on the couch, with Boomer lying on the floor beside her.

Now morning light was beaming through the window. Lizzie could smell coffee and — was that bacon? The screeching continued as Lizzie pulled on her robe and ran downstairs. What had Boomer done now? She couldn't even imagine.

When she ran into the kitchen, full of apologies, she realized that the screeching sound was Risa. The Fab Four were sitting around the table, sipping coffee and staring at Risa as she babbled out a story between braying peals of laughter. "So he waits until I'm asleep, right?" Risa was saying. "And then I guess the papers must have slipped out of my hand, and he decides to make himself a little bed out of them." She held up a handful of papers. Some were shredded, some were soaked with drool, and all of them left a trail of dog hair as Risa merrily waved them around, braying at the top of her lungs.

Mom shooed the flying hairs away from her

coffee mug. "And — you're laughing?" she asked. "I'd be furious if he messed up something I'd been working on."

Joy put a hand on Risa's arm. "Are you okay, honey?" she asked.

Risa just kept laughing.

Annie just shook her head and said aloud what they were all thinking: "The girl's gone crazy."

Lizzie bit her lip. She should have been more careful! She should have kept Boomer away from Risa. Now Mom's friend was hysterical, and it was obvious that nobody knew what to do.

"Risa, please," Joy said. Now she was standing behind Risa, massaging her friend's shoulders in an effort to calm her down. "Get a grip, honey. It's just a report. You can print it out again, can't you?"

Risa couldn't stop laughing long enough to answer. Finally, she caught her breath. "That's exactly the point," she said. "It's just a report. A report" — she waved the papers again — "that's nothing but a huge waste of time. The client who ordered it is going ahead with their silly plan no matter what I tell them. I don't even like these people. I don't like most of the people I work with. All they care about is money, money, money."

She took a deep breath, then grinned down at Boomer, who lay at her feet looking up at her as if she were the Queen of the Dogs. "It took this crazy messy wild dog to make me realize that I am way overdue for a big change. This life I'm living? Fancy restaurants and designer clothes and constant travel? It's not for me. I've made enough money. I can quit and take some time to think about what I want to do next. I can . . . and I'm going to. Starting right now." She smiled around at her friends as she smacked the table. "This minute."

"Yes!" Annie hollered, holding up her hand for a high five. "So where will you go? What will you do?"

"Actually," Risa said, looking down at her coffee mug, "I was wondering about that cabin of yours. The old bunkhouse. Is it — is it available?"

"Are you kidding?" Annie jumped up and threw her arms around Risa. "I'd love to have you there. You could help out on the ranch, ride horses every day, feed the chickens, all of it."

"And . . . do you think there might be room for Boomer, too?" Risa asked.

Annie stared at her. "Boomer?"

"I think he's just what I need," Risa told her friend. "I knew it the minute he put his muddy paws on me in the van that day. You said to look into his eyes and I did, and suddenly I didn't care one bit about mud, or drool, or any of it. I realized that I *need* a little more mess in my life. I need this guy." She pointed at the big puppy by her feet. "He knew it, too. I think I just had to convince myself — and everybody else — that I was the right person for him." She reached down to scratch between Boomer's ears, and his tail thumped on the floor.

I'd go anywhere with you!

Risa looked at Lizzie. "Remember when you said that thing about how I would be a great dog owner? That's when everything clicked into place. Of course I would! I watched you training him in the backyard. I can do that! I mean, I started my own business. I should be able to teach a dog this smart and sweet how to behave."

"Well, there's no question that he'll make your life messier," Mom said.

"And better in every way," Lizzie added. She could not stop grinning as she pictured Risa and Boomer together at Annie's ranch. She never would have guessed it when she first met Mom's friends, but this really was the perfect match. Boomer had made the right choice after all when he fell in love with Risa. Lizzie could already tell that the two of them were going to live happily ever after.

PUPPY TIPS

Do you like to vacuum, brush and bathe a dog, and constantly clean up muddy tracks? If you can learn to love these things, a dog like Boomer might be the perfect match for you! If not, you might want to think about a smaller, short-haired dog. Some people fall in love with the look of a certain breed but may not be prepared for the reality of caring for a dog who sheds, barks, or has a lot of energy. Taking care of any dog is a big responsibility, but some dogs are more of a challenge than others. Still, for the love of a dog like Boomer, it might be worth all the trouble!

Dear Reader,

Every March I like to help my neighbors collect sap from their maple trees. We boil it down to make delicious maple syrup. One year, another helper brought along her dog, a big fluffy white lovebug. She told me his story: He had grown up in the wild, the biggest in a litter of abandoned puppies. He had learned to live in a house, but he still had funny habits, like sometimes staying out all night, barking his head off. I loved his story and always wanted to write about a puppy like him. That's how this book got its start.

Yours from the Puppy Place,
Ellen Miles

P.S. If you like reading about big dogs, check out MOOSE.

THE PUPPY PLACE
Where every puppy finds a home

MOOSE

ELLEN MILES

SCHOLASTIC

ABOUT THE AUTHOR

Ellen Miles loves dogs, which is why she has a great time writing the Puppy Place books. And guess what? She loves cats, too! (In fact, her very first pet was a beautiful tortoiseshell cat named Jenny.) That's why she came up with the Kitty Corner series. Ellen lives in Vermont and loves to be outdoors every day, walking, biking, skiing, or swimming, depending on the season. She also loves to read, cook, explore her beautiful state, play with dogs, and hang out with friends and family.

Visit Ellen at www.ellenmiles.net.

THE PUPPY PLACE

DON'T MISS THE
NEXT PUPPY PLACE
ADVENTURE!

Here's a peek at DAISY!

"Good day, honey?" Mom asked.

Charles thought for a second. That wasn't such an easy question to answer. He had liked the cupcakes, and the Valentines. He didn't like remembering the look on Luke's face as he stared down at that card. He shrugged.

"Okay, then," said Mom. Sometimes she understood when Charles didn't feel like talking. She started the van and drove up the street. "Aren't you going to ask me where we're going?"

"Dentist?" Charles asked. "Eye doctor?" He didn't remember having an appointment, but that was nothing new.

"Try 'puppy'," Mom said.

Charles stared at her. "Puppy?" he asked.

She nodded. "Looks like we have a new dog to foster." She grinned at him. "So, *now* is it a good day?"

Charles stared at his mom. "Sure it's good," he said. "But where's the puppy coming from?"

Mom sighed. "It's kind of a long story, but remember my friend Wilma who works at the paper?"

"The lady at the front desk?" Charles loved to visit the *Littleton News* offices with his mom. It was pretty cool that she was a reporter for the local newspaper, even if she did mostly write about boring stuff like school board meetings or town budget issues. He always liked seeing her name underneath a headline: By Betsy Peterson.

"Right, she's the receptionist. She's worked there for longer than anyone else, even the editor." Mom shook her head. "Wilma could probably put out that newspaper all by herself if she had to. Anyway, she's been telling me for a while about this new puppy her daughter was going to get."

"What kind?" Charles asked.

Mom thought for a second. "Some kind of terrier? I can't remember for sure. It's a little dog, I know that. And very cute, apparently."

Mom was really more of a cat person, so it wasn't surprising she hadn't paid attention to the puppy's breed. Charles smiled. He liked little dogs. Lizzie was into the big breeds, but Charles loved a puppy who could fit on your lap, or be carried around. "So, did they get it?" he asked.